NICHOLAS HELLER

Goblins in Green

PICTURES BY
JOS. A. SMITH

A MULBERRY PAPERBACK BOOK • NEW YORK

Gouache, watercolor paints, and colored pencils were used for the full-color art.
The text type is Seagull Medium.

The Library of Congress has cataloged the Greenwillow Books edition of
Goblins in Green as follows:
Heller, Nicholas.
Goblins in green / by Nicholas Heller ; pictures by Jos. A. Smith.
p. cm.
Summary: A succession of goblins, from Annabelle in an amber blouse to Zelda in
a zebra anorak, presents the letters of the alphabet.
ISBN 0-688-12802-5 (trade). ISBN 0-688-12803-3 (lib. bdg.)
[1. Alphabet. 2. Goblins—Fiction. 3. Color—Fiction.]
I. Smith, Jos. A. (Joseph Anthony) (date), ill. II. Title. PZ7.H37426Go
1995 [E]—dc20 94-4575 CIP AC

1 3 5 7 9 10 8 6 4 2
First Mulberry Edition, 1999
ISBN 0-688-17058-7

FOR JOSIE
AND ALLIE
—N. H.

FOR CHARISSA,
WITH LOVE
—J. A. S.

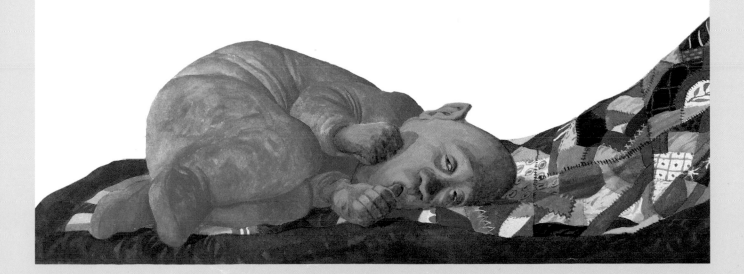

Take a peek through the trap door.
What do you see?
Ghastly green goblins getting dressed
in clothes from A to Z.
Look!

Annabelle is attired in an amber blouse,

and Bedford is wearing bright blue chinos.

Clara clowns in
cranberry dungarees,

and **D**esmond has donned
denim earmuffs.

Eloise is enthralled with her emerald frock,

Frieda has found
some flowered gloves,

and Gwendolyn grabs
a green gabardine hat.

Henderson hobbles horribly
on ice skates,

as **I**gnatius inspects
an indigo jersey.

Jared jumps in his
jaunty knickers,

and **K**entigern kicks in his
king-sized leotard.

Lobelia lazes in a leopard mackintosh.

Morgana is modeling a multicolored nightgown.

Norbert is nimble in
some nifty overalls,

and **O**sbert oversleeps in his orange pajamas.

Percival parades in
a patchwork quilt,

and quarrelsome Quentin
has on a quilted robe.

Renata looks regal in her red sarong.

Selwin is sporting sorrel trousers.

Thompson is trying some tulip underwear,

while **U**lrika unlooses
her unusual veil.

Vincent looks vile in his violet woolies.

Whatever **W**endell wears will have to be eXtra-large!

Xerxes looks eXemplary in an eXtraordinary yoke.

Yolanda yodels in a
yellow zoot suit,

and just look at Zelda,
zipped in her zebra anorak!

But speak softly while
you're peeking.
Don't let the goblins hear!
If you make the slightest sound,
they all will disappear!